MiJos

FIELD TRIP TROUBLE

THE MIJOS ARE UP
ON WHAT'S GOING DOWN!
CHECK OUT THEIR
OTHER AWESOME ADVENTURES!

WHO DAT?
THE OFFICIAL MIJOS™ HANDBOOK

#1 THE FIESTA FACE-OFF
#2 SAVE MIJO PARK
#3 SPOOKY'S NIGHTMARE

From the creator of the HOMIES®

FIELD TRIP TROUBLE
BY DAVID GONZALES

Scholastic Inc.

New York Toronto London Auckland Sydney
Mexico City New Delhi Hong Kong Buenos Aires

TO MY PARENTS, ANDY AND DEE-DEE.
THEY ALWAYS ENCOURAGED MY TALENT,
WHICH ALLOWED ME TO FOLLOW MY DREAM.

ISBN 0-439-56803-X
MIJOS and all related characters are trademarks of HOMIESHOP.
Copyright © 2005 HOMIESHOP.
All rights reserved.

A special condensed version of this book is being published as MIJOS: FRISCO FIELD TRIP.

12 11 10 9 8 7 6 5 4 3 2 1   5 6 7 8 9 10/0

Printed in the U.S.A.
First printing, November 2005

WHO DAT?

GET TO KNOW THE MIJOS™!

ANDRES
A.K.A. LIL DRE

JULIAN
A.K.A. BUBBA

ANTONIO
A.K.A. BABY BOY

ESTEBAN
A.K.A. SPOOKY

SEÑORA CAMPOS

BERNARO
A.K.A. BENNIE

REGGIE
A.K.A. REAL SHORT

SELENA
A.K.A. RAGDOLL

MARIA
A.K.A. BABYDOLL

ANGELA
A.K.A. ANGEL BABY

JJ

MONICA
A.K.A. HUERA

SALVADOR
A.K.A. SAL

BRIAN
A.K.A. B-DOWN

MIGUEL
A.K.A. MOUSY

PEDRO
A.K.A. PE

TABLE OF CONTENTS

THE BUS STOP

Andres sat alone at the bus stop as the sun came up behind the buildings across the street. He was so excited about today's class field trip that he'd arrived at the bus stop extra early. Lil Dre, as everyone called him, was an "early bird." Dre's dad liked to say, "The early bird catches the worm." That meant that it paid to be early, and that's what Lil Dre was all the time — early. Especially on a day like today!

Lil Dre's teacher, Señora Campos, had worked hard to plan a field trip for the kids in her class at Oaktown Elementary School. Everyone called Dre and his friends the Mijos, which means "my children." They were a good group, worked hard, and all looked out for one another. As a reward, Señora Campos wanted to take the class out on the road to see the different places they had been learning about in school. Since their latest unit was state history, the Mijos were headed across the bay to San Francisco for their field trip! What better way to learn about California than to explore one of its most popular cities?

Lil Dre had ridden through San Francisco in a car before, but had never visited it for real. All he knew was that the city was the home of the Forty-Niners, the Giants, and the Golden Gate Bridge. The idea of seeing a new city for himself was exciting, and Dre could hardly wait to get started! But the Mijos always seemed to cause so much trouble in class that Dre wondered if this field trip would turn into another wild Mijos adventure.

A voice rang out from behind him, snapping Lil Dre out of his daydream. "Hey, *you're* early!"

Lil Dre turned around to see Baby Boy, one of his main Mijo pals, walking toward him. Baby Boy was easy to spot because he had a big shiny bald head! It looked a little bit like a bowling ball sometimes.

"What's up, Lil Dre?" asked Baby Boy. He sat down next to Dre on the bus stop bench. This was the official Mijos bus stop, right down the street from Mijo Park. The school bus would pick them up here for their field trip.

"It's all good," Dre said. He smiled, kind of embarrassed. "I couldn't sleep, so I got here a little early."

Baby Boy laughed. "Yeah, right!" he said. "You don't have to lie to kick it with me, bro. You're *always* early."

Lil Dre couldn't help but laugh, too. The two boys shook hands and banged knuckles. Nobody knew Lil Dre like Baby Boy. That's why they were best buds.

It wasn't long before a white pickup truck pulled up to the bus stop, and Selena climbed out. You could spot her big bright eyes and long black braids from a mile away. She blew a kiss to her *papi*, Pepe. Pepe waved to Lil Dre and Baby Boy as he drove off.

Selena walked up and sat on the other side of Lil Dre. She was happy to see the boys there. *"Buenas días!"* she said.

"Good morning!" said Lil Dre, smiling.

"You're the first girl to show up," Baby Boy said matter-of-factly.

"Cool," said Selena. "I was hoping I wouldn't be the first person here. If you guys hadn't been here already, my *papi* wouldn't have let me wait by myself."

Selena put her backpack on the ground, next to Lil Dre and Baby Boy's bags. That's where they kept important things like snacks, lunch, bottled water, and extra stuff to keep them busy on the bus. Dre had brought a drawing pad, pencils, and an eraser. He liked to draw whenever he had a chance, especially when he saw something cool and unique. He was sure that the Mijos would see lots of cool stuff on their field trip!

Suddenly, the three Mijos heard a thumping sound in the distance, getting closer and closer. *Btoo-btang, btoo-btang, boom-boom, ba-boom.* That sound could only mean one thing — B-Down and Real Short were here! Real Short was an African-American kid who lived in the Mijos' neighborhood. He had all sorts of style, and wanted to be a record producer someday, like Dr. Dre. His real name was Reggie, but because he was kind of small for his age, the Mijos called

him Real Short. He didn't seem to mind. B-Down was the little Irish kid who always came down from the Oakland hills to hang out with the Mijos. His real name was Brian Downey, but B-Down was his rapper name. He didn't go to school with the rest of the Mijos. Since his family lived in a nicer area, B-Down went to a private school. But he hung around the 'hood with his Mijos friends because he was "keeping it real." Señora Campos had invited him along on their field trip, with his parents' permission.

Lil Dre could see Real Short and B-Down walking down the street toward the bus stop, rapping like crazy. That's what the noise had been!

Throw yo' hands in the air
Act like ya just don't care;
These two rhymin' Mijos are in yo' face,
We're 'bout to head to San Fran and bounce
    up outta this place!

Dre, Baby Boy, and Selena greeted the rappers with a round of applause. Real Short and B-Down bowed and pointed to their fans as they got to the bus stop. They loved getting props.

Bubba wasn't far behind. He walked up, acting like he owned the place. In a way, he did. Bubba was the big Mijos bully, and he usually got exactly what he wanted.

"What's up, Dre?" he asked. "What's up, Baby Boy? How's it going, Selena?" Then Bubba turned to Real Short and B-Down. "What's up, Pete and Repeat?" he asked, sneering. He liked their raps but always made it clear that he thought Real Short and B-Down were a couple of rapping fools.

Lil Dre changed the subject before Bubba could pick a fight. "Can you believe it, Bubba? We're going to the City by the Bay today. San Francisco! How cool is that?"

"Man, I don't want to go on this dumb field trip," Bubba grumbled. "There are just gonna be even more rules than usual — *boring*!" Bubba always talked tough and tried to act like he didn't care, but deep down, Dre figured, Bubba had to be excited about the field trip.

"But it'll still be cool to see the city, don't you think?" Baby Boy chimed in.

Bubba wasn't convinced. "The only reason I'm coming at all is because Señora Campos said that missing a field trip is like cutting school," he said. "Then I'd get in trouble. Fine. I'll show *her* trouble. I'll cause so much trouble on this field trip, Señora Campos will be sorry she made me come!"

Lil Dre frowned. "You shouldn't do that," he said. "Señora Campos is nice. I'm sure she just wants you to have fun with the rest of us."

Lil Dre liked Señora Campos. She always gave him a lot of attention, and said that Dre was a natural-born leader. She told him that he should use that quality to help the other Mijos do the right thing in different situations. Dre didn't want to let her down now!

Pretty soon, a whole bunch of the Mijos started

to arrive, since it was almost time to leave. Spooky, Mousy, Pedro, Sal, and Bennie all walked up to the bus stop together, and Maria, Monica, and Angela weren't far behind.

"Where's Señora Campos?" Spooky asked.

"I don't know. We're supposed to leave at nine," Dre said. "The bus isn't here yet, either. They only have ten minutes!"

"Maybe the trip is canceled," said Spooky, his eyes wide. "Maybe there was a big earthquake in San Francisco, and the city was destroyed, so they decided not to go today."

Lil Dre tried not to laugh. Spooky had a really crazy imagination. But Bubba didn't think Spooky's idea was so weird.

"YEAHHHHHHHH!" shouted Bubba. "The field trip is canceled!"

CHAPTER 2

BUS TROUBLE

Screeeeech!

Suddenly, a shiny red car pulled up just in front of the bus stop. It was really cool, like Lil Dre's dream car! It was painted candy-apple red with white rally stripes, and it had dark tinted windows so Dre couldn't see who was inside. The engine had a loud, deep throbbing sound, like it was ready to race.

"Oooh, check out that Corvette," said Bennie. "I'll bet that baby has a 454 big-block high-performance engine in it!"

Bennie's dad owned Hilltop Auto Shop, and he hung out there every day after school. He knew a lot about cars. *If Bennie's impressed by this car, it must be* really *sweet,* Lil Dre thought.

The car door suddenly swung open and loud salsa music drifted out into the air. A familiar figure climbed out. She was holding a purse in one hand and balancing a large cup of coffee in the other. It was Señora Campos! She closed and locked the car door behind her with a *beep beep* from her remote. Then she walked toward the group with her big, familiar smile.

"Good morning, and how are the Mijos today?" she asked.

"Good morning, Señora Campos!" the kids all called out. None of them knew she had such a cool car! They were really happy to see her. Most of them, anyway.

"Are you guys all ready to explore the big city today?" Señora Campos asked, her voice full of excitement.

"Yeahhh!" came the reply from all of the Mijos . . . except for Bubba. He yelled, "NOOOO!" while waving his arms in the air like he was cheering. *It's going to be a long day if Bubba keeps acting like this*, Lil Dre thought.

Señora Campos just ignored Bubba. She and the Mijos had learned long ago that that was the best thing to do with him. "Wait a minute." She looked around, puzzled. "Where's the school bus?"

"It's not here yet," said Lil Dre.

"Yeah, so we all need to go home," added Bubba.

"We heard there was a big earthquake that destroyed San Francisco, so that's probably why the bus isn't coming," added Spooky. "Is that true, Señora Campos?"

"Of course not," their teacher replied. "We would know if there was a big earthquake — we would have felt it here, too! No, there wasn't an earthquake, but JJ should definitely be here with the bus by now." With that, Señora Campos grabbed her phone from her purse, flipped the lid open, and began dialing.

After a quick conversation, Señora Campos turned back to the Mijos. "JJ thought he was supposed to pick us up at the school yard. He'll be here in just a few minutes."

"Yeahhh!" the Mijos cried. Bubba chimed in with a loud "Booooooo!"

Lil Dre looked at Bubba and smiled. Something told Dre that Bubba would have fun on their field trip, whether he wanted to or not. Lil Dre just hoped he was right!

A few minutes later, the bus pulled up with a hiss and a screech. It was a gigantic yellow school bus with big shiny chrome wheels. JJ's bus was the coolest-looking school bus on the road. The word "OAKTOWN" was written down the sides, and it cruised along on wide, low-profile tires.

By now, the Mijos were all jumping around.

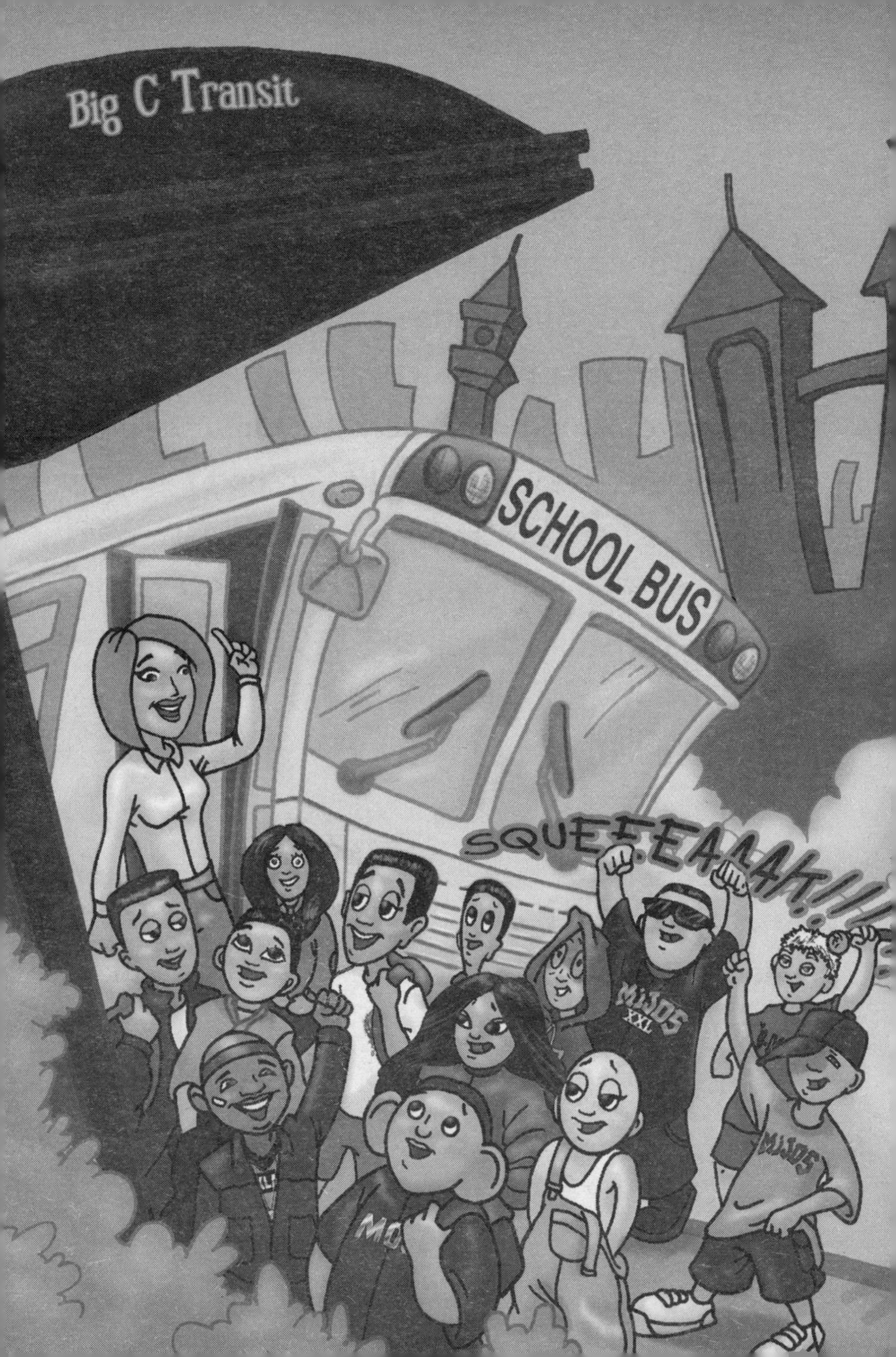
Big C Transit
SCHOOL BUS
SQUEEEAAAK!!!
MIJOS
XXL
MIJOS

They were ready to get going! Bubba stood off to one side. His hands were shoved in his pockets, and he had a sour look on his face. Señora Campos gathered everyone around and began a short lecture.

"Okay, everyone, settle down now. I want you to board the bus in an orderly fashion, find a seat, and behave. You know that JJ takes a lot of pride in his bus, so treat it right. I'm going to go grab the permission slips from my car, and I expect you all to be seated when I get on the bus." With that, she turned and walked away.

Before anyone knew what was happening, Bubba suddenly yelled, "Last one on the bus is a rotten egg!"

There was a mad rush toward the bus. Everyone was pushing and laughing, and Bubba was the loudest of all. "She's gonna wish she didn't make me come on this dumb field trip!" he snickered.

Once they got on the bus, Lil Dre saw that Mousy tried to push Sal out of the way so he could get the seat all the way in the back. Sal looked determined to get that same seat. Suddenly, the two boys were rolling on the floor, fighting. Sal and Mousy rolled over and over, hanging on to each other and not letting go. Sal had a grip on each of Mousy's big round ears, and Mousy held on to Sal's shoulders.

"Fight! Fight! Fight!" The chant started immediately, as everyone piled on the bus to watch. Maria yelled for them to stop — she hated fights. But Mousy and Sal weren't really fighting. It was more like wrestling. JJ tried to tell the kids to settle down, but everyone was too riled up to listen. B-Down had started rapping again. Real Short was beatboxing: *bumpety-bump-bump boom.* Bubba egged Mousy and Sal on.

"Here comes Señora Campos!" said Lil Dre, looking out the bus window. "Stop! You guys are gonna get in trouble."

It was too late.

"There will be no fighting on this bus!" Señora Campos yelled, climbing the bus steps. "Stop it — immediately!"

Mousy and Sal let go of each other at the same time. They could tell by her voice that Señora Campos really meant business.

"Now, you two shake hands and make up," Señora Campos continued. "I thought you were good friends. Friends don't fight."

Mousy and Sal looked at each other suspiciously for a minute. Neither one answered Señora Campos. They knew better than to tell her that Bubba started it by making everyone race to the bus. Instead, with embarrassed looks on their faces, the two boys shook hands. They walked to the back of the bus together and decided to share the seat, since they could both fit.

Right away, Bubba walked up to them. "I don't think so," he said. He snapped his fingers and pointed to a different seat.

Both boys knew what Bubba wanted. They got up and moved right away, rather than causing more trouble. Bubba had been a bully since they were all in kindergarten. He was much bigger than the rest of the Mijos, so no one ever really challenged him. Lil Dre was the only one who could get him under control sometimes, and that was just because Bubba happened to think that Dre was cool.

Once everyone was seated, Señora Campos took one last head count and gave JJ the okay to head out. JJ popped in his favorite CD, and the music filled the bus. *How awesome that JJ's the one driving us on our first field trip!* Lil Dre thought.

Dre settled in his seat and stared out the window as the bus headed west toward San Francisco Bay. You could sometimes see San Francisco's tall skyscrapers from parts of Oaktown, especially up in the hills where B-Down lived. Lil Dre remembered the time that B-Down had a huge barbeque at his house and had invited all of the Mijos. They played games in his game room, swam in his pool, shot hoops on his basketball court, and rode go-carts on his grand prix racetrack. B-Down's gigantic house was like an amusement park — but everything was free! That night, the Mijos had camped out in his backyard, and they saw all the lights of San Francisco. Dre thought it looked like a magical city, like the Land of Oz or something. And now he was going to see it up close!

Just then, the bus slowed to a stop. "Uh-oh," JJ said. "Traffic jam." Through the window, Lil Dre saw a sea of honking cars all around them. *This field trip might be over before it even begins,* Dre thought sadly. They were stuck!

CHAPTER 3

A SAN FRAN SHORTCUT

After a moment, JJ turned around in the driver's seat. "Well, Mijos," he said, "we're gonna have a hard time getting to San Francisco this way." All of the kids groaned loudly . . . all except for Bubba, of course.

"Lucky for us, I know another way to the city!" JJ continued. With that, he pulled off the highway at the nearest exit, made a U-turn, and got back on the highway heading north. "How many of you have been across the Golden Gate Bridge?" he asked.

A few hands went up in the air, and the rest of the Mijos whispered excitedly.

"Well," JJ continued, "for those of you who haven't, you're going to today. We're taking the Golden Gate Bridge to San Francisco!"

"Yeahhh!!" The Mijos' shout echoed throughout the bus. *What a great way to start the trip!* Lil Dre thought.

It was a beautiful day, and there was lots to see as the bus approached the Golden Gate Bridge. Señora Campos stood at the front of the bus and called out all sorts of cool facts about the bridge as it got closer and closer. After all, this trip was about learning state history — though that was easy to forget with all of the excitement.

"The Golden Gate Bridge is a suspension cable bridge," she started. "When it was built, the span between its towers was the farthest of any bridge of its kind in the world. You can imagine how difficult it must have been to make. It took a long time, and was quite dangerous. A lot of people even died during its construction."

"How did they die?" Spooky asked immediately. He always looked for the scary element in every story. "Did they fall off the top while they were working? Did sharks in the water eat them?"

"I'm not exactly sure," Señora Campos responded.

"Ooooh!" Spooky said. "But it might have happened! It would be crazy to see a real shark up close."

"You just might," answered Señora Campos, smiling. "Don't forget that we're going to the aquarium this afternoon. But let's get back to the bridge." By now, the bus was passing over the bridge, and the Mijos peered through the windows down at the water below. "This is one of the most popular tourist sites in the entire world. Now, who knows what that building is?" she asked, pointing out the window at a tall, triangular skyscraper in the middle of the city, straight ahead on the other side of the bridge.

"That's the pyramid building!" said Maria. "My daddy does business there sometimes."

"Correct," answered Señora Campos. "That is the Trans America building, but it's also called the pyramid building because of its resemblance to an Egyptian pyramid. It's become one of the most recognized landmarks in San Francisco."

"I wonder if there are mummies buried in there, maybe in the basement or something," said Spooky. He was spooking himself out more by the minute.

"Now, take it easy, Spooky," Señora Campos said, laughing. She knew all about Spooky's fascination with scary stories, and she tried to help him keep it under control. She always told him that it was great to have an active imagination, but that he couldn't let it take over *all* the time.

From the backseat, Bubba added, "There can't be a mummy there, dummy. It's not even a real pyramid. Everyone knows that."

Spooky didn't say anything in response, but Señora Campos did. "I won't have that bully attitude on this bus, Bubba. Now apologize to Spooky," she said.

Bubba snickered. "Okay, Spooky, I'm sorry," he began. Señora Campos nodded and turned her head away, but Bubba wasn't finished. He hissed at Spooky, so that Señora Campos couldn't hear, "Sorry that you're such a big scaredy cat!"

"Just ignore him, Spooky," Lil Dre said. Spooky did just that. He didn't even turn around to look at Bubba. If he had, Bubba would have been able to see that he'd hurt Spooky's feelings. Instead, B-Down started up a rap, to distract Bubba and keep him from picking on Spooky. Immediately, Real Short began beatboxing. He was always on cue!

B-Down began:

Señora Campos teach it to us, try to tell us
  how to live,
Spreading all her knowledge. She's got so much
  to give!
Bubba doesn't like this field trip, but we sure
  glad he came.
It's true that without Bubba, the Mijos aren't
  the same.

Bubba liked that line. He gave B-Down a high-five and settled back in his seat. He was done picking on the other Mijos . . . for now.

CHAPTER 4

HITTIN' THE STREETS

The bus cruised through the financial district of San Francisco, and all of the Mijos strained to peer out the windows. Bubba sat low in his seat, staring at the ceiling of the bus.

"Look at these giant skyscrapers!" said Lil Dre, craning his neck. "You can't even see the tops of them from here."

"Can we walk around and look at the big buidings?" Baby Boy called out.

"Yeah," Monica chimed in. "Can we, Señora Campos?"

"I don't see why not," Señora Campos said. "We have a few minutes to spare, since we took a shortcut!" She turned to JJ. "Could you pull over right up there?"

"My pleasure, Señora," JJ answered. He pulled off on the side of the street and opened the bus doors with a mechanical hiss. The Mijos piled out of the bus in a hurry, excited to stretch their legs and see the sights.

Bubba was the last one off the bus. He was in no hurry. "Who cares about some big boring buildings?" he grumbled.

"Okay, here we go!" called Señora Campos, heading along the sidewalk. The Mijos followed close behind, their heads swiveling to look up at the tall skyscrapers.

"Looking up at those buildings makes me dizzy!" said Bennie. "How did they build them all?"

"Good question, Bennie!" Señora Campos answered. "Architects and engineers designed those buildings very carefully, using a lot of precise math and measurements. Then they hired construction companies to build them. You're great at math, Bennie. Do you think you'd like to be an engineer someday?"

"Yeah!" Bennie said. "Designing buildings would rock!"

"And you could hire me to come and paint murals on them," Lil Dre added. All of the Mijos knew Dre was the best artist around.

As the group continued down the street, they began passing all kinds of different buildings. There were camera stores, restaurants, delis, art galleries, fancy clothing stores, and even a few museums.

"Ouch!" came a sudden yell from the back of

the pack. It was Selena, and she was looking at Bubba angrily.

Señora Campos looked back at her. "What's wrong, Selena?"

Selena rubbed the side of her head. "Nothing, Señora. I just stubbed my toe on the curb, that's all." She shot Bubba another dirty look as Señora Campos moved on. Lil Dre had a feeling Selena wasn't telling the truth. Bubba loved pulling on her braids, just to annoy her. It drove Selena crazy, but she would never tell on Bubba. She didn't want to make him angry. *I'd better keep an eye on Bubba,* Lil Dre thought. *He's up to more trouble than usual today, and Señora Campos has her hands full on this trip already!*

The group looped around the block and walked a bit farther, then back to the bus. When the door swung open, the air conditioning on the bus felt refreshing. *Boy,* thought Lil Dre, *JJ really knows how to roll.*

Once everyone was on board, the bus cruised through the Mission District. Señora Campos told them that was where a lot of the city's Latino population lived and hung out. The shops all had signs in front of them in Spanish that said things like *mercado*, *tienda*, *panadería*, and *musica*.

"Look at those cool murals!" said Dre. He pointed at a large, colorful wall with a painting of an Aztec warrior in front of an Aztec sun calendar. Dre was proud of his Mexican heritage and loved learning about the Aztecs. "Can we get out and look at them, Señora Campos?"

"I'm afraid that right now we have a ferry to catch," Señora Campos said. "Remember, our first stop is Alcatraz Island to visit the famous prison!"

Once again, shouts of excitement went up from the Mijos. Even Bubba smiled a little. *Uh-oh*, thought Lil Dre. *Bubba could get into all sorts of trouble at Alcatraz!*

The bus turned down a busy street along the water's edge. The water was lined with giant buildings, which had numbered signs on them: PIER 43, PIER 42, PIER 41, and so on. The piers were already getting really crowded with tourists.

"Here we are, Pier 39," said JJ. He pulled the bus into a parking spot. It had barely come to a stop before the Mijos were pushing to get off. They couldn't wait to explore the pier!

CHAPTER 5

A SECRET PLAN

O nce the Mijos all clambered off the bus, Señora Campos gave them some instructions. "Okay, kids," she said. "I'm going to the ticket booth to get our tickets for the tour of Alcatraz. It might take a little while because the line looks awfully long. You kids can explore the pier for a while, but I need you to stick together, and stay with JJ. I'll be able to see you from my spot in line, so no misbehaving!" Señora Campos looked right at Bubba when she said that last part. She seemed to know just what Bubba was thinking.

The pier was full of shops and performers. Mimes, break-dancers, and magicians all had huge crowds gathered around them on the pier. Whenever they finished a performance, the people who had watched put some change into the cups, hats, and buckets that the performers held out. Lil Dre had heard of street performers but had never seen them before. Most of them were really talented!

JJ led the Mijos in and out of poster shops, clothing shops, souvenir shops, and even ice-cream shops. There was a lot of cool stuff to see. Some of the kids had brought money to buy souvenirs. In one of the stores, Lil Dre found a postcard of the Aztec mural he'd seen from the bus. He bought it with some of the spending money his dad had given him and put it in his backpack. He couldn't wait to get home and try to paint his own version!

As he turned from the counter, Lil Dre saw Bubba standing just outside the door of the store, whispering to B-Down and Real Short. *What is Bubba up to now?* he thought. Whatever it was, Dre was pretty sure it was going to get someone in trouble!

Lil Dre walked quietly over to the door, making sure that Bubba couldn't see him. He stood in the doorway and tried to listen to what they were talking about.

"I'll bet we can get some of these tourists to put lots of money into our hats," Bubba whispered.

"I'm not so sure about this, Bubba," B-Down said.

"Yeah," said Real Short. "Won't we get in trouble?"

"Nah," Bubba scoffed. "All you're doing is rapping, just like you always do. But now, if these people like what they hear, they'll give us some cash! There's nothing wrong with that. I'll be like your business manager. And since I'm your business manager, you have to do what I say."

Señora Campos isn't going to like this, Lil Dre thought. He looked over his shoulder into the store. JJ and the rest of the Mijos were still looking at the souveniers. *What do I do?*

But he didn't have time to think of a plan before Bubba yelled out, "That's right! Come hear the rappin' kids from Oaktown!" He took off his hat and stood back along the wall, ready to collect change from the crowd after the performance. B-Down and Real Short busted into a rap:

Serious biz, peoples, believe it or not!
Some of us don't have what you've all got.
You may think it's all really funny,
But we ain't laughing, cuz we ain't got no
    money.

As they continued on, a crowd started to form.

They didn't get much farther before a voice rang out from the crowd. "What is going on here?" Señora Campos pushed through, and she did not look happy. The crowd drifted away, and B-Down and Real Short looked ashamed. Bubba stood off to the side, annoyed that his plan had been foiled before he collected any money.

"Reggie? Brian? What do you think you're doing?" Señora Campos asked.

The boys were at a loss for words. "We ... um ... I didn't ... ," Reggie mumbled.

"What you just did was completely unacceptable!" Señora Campos said sternly. "The performers along this pier are professionals. They have permits to perform here. You know that it's wrong to collect money like that, when you don't have a right to."

Real Short and B-Down hung their heads. They glanced over at Bubba but didn't say anything. Lil Dre could tell they didn't want to make him mad. Bubba already gave them a hard enough time!

"We'll discuss your punishment on the bus this afternoon," Señora Campos continued. "In the meantime, you two are to stay near me for the rest of the trip."

That's not fair! thought Lil Dre. *I'll have to tell Señora Campos what really happened, before she gives B-Down and Real Short their punishment. Even if it makes Bubba mad, it's the right thing to do.* But not even Lil Dre was brave enough to rat out Bubba right in front of his face!

CHAPTER 6

ACROSS THE BAY

Just then, the ferry pulled into the boat dock, sounding its horn.

"Come on, Mijos!" Señora Campos called, leaning into the store. "It's time to go!"

Everyone filed out of the store, talking excitedly about all the cool stuff they'd seen. None of them had any idea that Bubba had just caused so much trouble, except for Lil Dre.

Señora Campos handed out a ferry ticket and an awesome Alcatraz shirt to each of them. That part was a surprise, and it was the best one yet. The shirts were black-and-white-striped, like the ones real prisoners wore! The Mijos were ready to go. They all ran over to the huge double-decker boat that bobbed in the water nearby.

Most of the Mijos had never been on a boat before, so they handed their tickets over and ran up the bouncy wooden rope bridge onto the ferry. It was *huge* inside! The kids had to explore the entire boat, from top to bottom, before they decided as a group that the front was the place to be.

Once the horn sounded again, the boat headed out into the bay. The soft breeze became a strong wind as the boat sped up. The sun was shining, and the Mijos gathered along the railing to look out on the water. Everything looked even better from there. They saw ducks, seagulls, pelicans, and other birds flying and swimming by. As the boat pulled farther and farther from the pier, the kids

saw a bunch of fat sea lions happily sunbathing on some old wooden docks.

"Hey, remember the movie *Titanic?*" Lil Dre asked. He leaned against the boat railing and spread his arms wide, like he was flying, just like he'd seen in the movie.

Maria was impressed. "Cool, Dre," she said. "You're brave!"

Spooky was sitting a safe distance away. "Be careful, Dre!" he chimed in. "Being that close to the water, you could get eaten by great white sharks! You heard what happened to the guys that built the bridge, didn't you?" Dre knew Spooky was being silly, but he backed away from the railing, anyway, so his friend wouldn't have to worry.

As the ferry cut through the water, a woman's voice came over the PA system. She shared all sorts of cool facts about the bay, described the fish, birds, and other wildlife that inhabited it, and talked about the various bridges that crossed it. Now that the Mijos were out on the water, they could see the bridges even better than before. Earlier, they'd seen the Golden Gate Bridge from above, and now they could see it from below. *How cool is that?* thought Lil Dre.

The voice on the PA system continued. "We are now approaching the island of Alcatraz. Alcatraz is the Spanish word for 'pelican.' The Spaniards named the island Alcatraz because of all of the pelicans that lived here." Lil Dre looked over at Señora Campos, sitting next to Bubba, and he saw her smile. They were learning a lot today, and that made their teacher happy!

The ferry finally docked, and the Mijos walked out onto the island. A man in a tan suit was there to greet them. "Welcome to Alcatraz Island National Park!" he said, smiling.

CHAPTER 7

JAIL TIME

he man in the tan suit was the Mijos' tour guide. He led them into the prison, sharing facts about Alcatraz the whole time. None of the Mijos were surprised that Spooky had lots and lots of questions.

"Were there any famous criminals kept here?" Spooky asked.

The tour guide nodded. "We get that question

a lot," he said. "And yes, we did keep some of the worst criminals of the time here. The Birdman of Alcatraz was kept here. A movie was made about his life. Alcatraz also had the famous gangster Al Capone for a while."

Spooky wasn't finished yet. "Did anyone die here? Did anyone escape? Are the bars in the cells thick? Are there ghosts here?" The guide looked at Señora Campos, puzzled. Lil Dre could see that he didn't know which question to answer first.

Señora Campos smiled. "How about if we begin the tour, and you can see the prison up close for yourself, Spooky?"

Everyone was happy to agree. But before they could officially get started, the tour guide had one more thing to say. "I do want to warn you, especially the smaller kids in the group," he began, "that there is absolutely no playing around in the jail cells, and no running around in places that are closed off or not well lit. This is a very old building, and it can be dangerous. You must stay with the group at all times. Does everyone understand?" Lil Dre glanced around to see the rest of the Mijos nodding solemnly. But out of the corner of his eye, he could see that Bubba was looking down at the ground, a little smile on his face. *Uh-oh,* Lil Dre thought. *This could mean* more *trouble!*

As the group followed their tour guide, he told them the island had been occupied by Native Americans before the prison was built. The island had an interesting history, but the Mijos were more interested in checking out the brick walls, dark hallways, and jail cells. Some of the Mijos lingered toward the back of the group. It was fun touching the walls and rusty bars, and they liked trying to read the graffiti.

"Wow," Lil Dre whispered to Baby Boy. "This place is crazy!"

"I know," Baby Boy said. "It's hard to believe that prisoners could live in those tiny little cells. I bet they all tried to escape."

Suddenly, Bubba butted in. "I bet I could escape from Alcatraz," he said proudly. "I can swim pretty far."

"No, you couldn't!" said Sal. "A shark would mistake you for a big old sea lion and eat you!" Everyone within earshot started laughing.

Bubba wasn't amused. He walked up to the nearest cell door, grabbed the bars, and gave them a hard shake. Suddenly, there was a loud creaking sound and the cell door swung open. "Ooohhh, nice!" Bubba said, forgetting about Sal's joke — luckily for Sal. He turned to Spooky. "Check it out, Spooky, this cell is open!" While the others watched, Bubba walked right into the tiny six-by-ten jail cell. Spooky was close behind.

"Hey, guys," Lil Dre whispered, looking up ahead the rest of the group. "The tour guide said we had to stay away from the jail cells."

"Yeah," Baby Boy chimed in. He always had Dre's back. "You guys don't want to get in trouble, do you?"

But Bubba and Spooky weren't listening. "Man, I'd go nuts in a place like this," Bubba said, looking around.

"I'll bet there are ghosts in here," Spooky said.

Bubba raised his eyebrows. "Yeah, I think you're right," he said. "They probably died trying to escape. In fact, it looks like there's an escape tunnel right there, behind that plastered brick." He pointed at the lower back corner of the cell. "See, that patch doesn't match the rest of the walls. They definitely covered something up."

Spooky's eyes lit up. "Maybe you're right," he said.

Lil Dre wasn't sure what Bubba was up to, but he knew it couldn't be good. "Hey, Spooky! We're probably missing some cool stuff on the tour. Let's get outta here," he said.

"Yeah, in just a minute," Spooky replied absentmindedly. He walked closer and closer to the back corner of the cell, crouching down to take a closer look. Before he realized what was going on . . .

Slam!

The cell door banged shut, and Spooky was all alone in the cell! Bubba stood on the other side of the cell door, cracking up. But Spooky didn't think it was very funny. As usual, he was totally afraid!

"Guys, let me out!" he cried. "I don't want to be stuck in here alone!"

"Oh, don't worry," Bubba said, grinning. "You're not alone. I'm sure there's a ghost in there with you!" That made him laugh even harder than before.

Spooky had had enough. He began to scream at the top of his lungs. "Aaaahhhhh! Help me! Help! I'm trapped in the cell with a ghost!" He rattled the bars with his hands.

"Hang on, Spooky!" said Lil Dre. He struggled with the latch on the door, but it wouldn't budge.

It was too late. "What's going on here?" Señora Campos cried. "Spooky, what are you doing in there?"

"I'm locked in here with a ghost!" Spooky moaned.

The tour guide pushed through the crowd. "Okay, don't be silly, now," he said. "There's no ghost in there." He pulled out some rusty old keys. "Just relax, everybody. I have the master keys here." He stuck an old iron key in the lock, twisted, and the door swung open. Spooky was free! He ran out of the cell and kissed the cement floor.

Señora Campos was not amused. "Spooky, you heard the rules. Why did you disobey and go into the jail cell? Did someone put you up to this?"

Spooky looked over at Bubba, ready to tell Señora Campos how he'd been tricked, but Bubba looked back at Spooky and slammed his right fist into his open left hand. Spooky got the message. He didn't say anything. He just looked down at the floor in shame.

Señora Campos sighed. "Okay, we'll discuss your detention when we're back at school. I expect excellent behavior from all of you for the rest of the day." She looked right at Bubba when she said that, and Lil Dre had a feeling that she knew Bubba was the one responsible for all the trouble on this field trip, even though no one would say so. "Right now, it's time to head back to the city and have some lunch."

With that, the Mijos thanked their tour guide and walked silently back to the ferry dock. *Well, at least things can only get better from here on,* Dre thought. *I mean, how much more trouble could Bubba cause?*

CHAPTER 8

WHAT'S FOR LUNCH?

After another ferry ride and a short trip on the school bus, the Mijos arrived in a shady park. It was picnic time!

"This is Golden Gate Park," announced Señora Campos from the front of the bus. "I know you all brought lunches, so grab them out of your backpacks and follow me!"

The kids grabbed their food, climbed down off

the bus, and walked across the freshly cut grass. They were exhausted from the excitement of the day, but there was something about the fresh air and sunshine that gave them new energy.

After a few minutes of walking, the group approached a big outdoor stage. It had a whole bunch of benches in front of it. Lil Dre recognized it right away. It was the big opera bandshell! Outdoor concerts and performances were held there when the weather was nice. It looked way bigger in real life than in the pictures Dre had seen.

"Okay, Mijos! Here we are. Pick a spot and enjoy your lunches," Señora Campos said. She sat down on a bench with JJ and pulled out a sandwich.

Lil Dre, Baby Boy, and Spooky sat off to one side by themselves. Dre opened his bag excitedly. He was hungry, and his dad always packed the best lunches! He pulled out a burrito, some apple juice, and some *pan dulce*, which was a type of sugary Mexican bread. He also had a banana and a little bag of potato chips. Baby Boy and Spooky had pretty awesome lunches, too, so the three boys had fun trading cookies, crackers, and chips back and forth.

It wasn't long before the fun was ruined, though. "Hey, guys! Bring your lunches over here." It was Bubba! Lil Dre turned around to see him taking first pick from everyone else's lunch.

No way! thought Dre. Luckily, he was a quick thinker. "Okay, Bubba, but all I have is soggy steamed spinach with some burned white rice. It's leftovers from last night's dinner."

Baby Boy followed his lead. "Yeah, all I have is a nasty baloney sandwich made out of the ends of the bread. The baloney looks like it has some green stuff growing on it, too."

Spooky was more honest. "I just have a tuna fish sandwich," he said. It was the truth, but all the Mijos knew that Bubba hated tuna fish.

"Yuck!" said Bubba. "Forget it! Besides, I've got some good stuff here." He continued asking for the best stuff out of everyone else's lunch. What

Bubba didn't know was that most of the kids were smart enough to bring a little something extra for him. They were used to his grubbing by now!

As soon as everyone was done eating, the Mijos picked up their trash, dumped it into the garbage cans, and headed back toward the bus. On their walk back through the park, they saw people doing slow-motion karate, throwing Frisbees, walking their dogs, sunbathing, riding bikes, and jogging. Lil Dre would have liked to stay there for a while, because there was so much cool stuff to do, but he knew that there was a lot more to see on their field trip.

Everyone hopped back on the bus, and Señora Campos counted heads to make sure that all the Mijos were present. Then she gave JJ the okay to roll out. "Next stop, Chinatown!" she said.

CHAPTER 9

THE GOLDEN DYNASTY

After a few minutes, the bus rolled through a really busy intersection. There were tons of little shops everywhere, and the streets were crammed with people. Even the traffic was bumper to bumper. It took JJ what seemed like forever just to find a spot to pull over and let the Mijos off the bus. *So this is Chinatown!* Lil Dre thought, looking around.

All sorts of different smells hit the Mijos as soon as they climbed down off the bus. People were yelling, laughing, talking, singing. Music was playing, horns were honking. There was so much going on, it was impossible to take it all in.

Señora Campos led the group down the street so they could see the sights. The first few blocks were all food shops, but they were nothing like the grocery stores that the Mijos were used to. Instead, these shops sold ducks, chickens, vegetables, spices, and baked goods. Some of the foods grossed the kids out a little bit, but others looked and smelled awesome.

After a few minutes, they came across a store that had a big red sign out front. It read Golden Dynasty Gift Shop in gold letters. "Should we check it out?" Señora Campos asked.

"Yeah!" came the reply from the Mijos. A bell jingled as they walked through the door.

The store was super-packed with cool stuff. There were glass statues, toys, kites, all kinds of

fun things to touch, and the Mijos made sure they touched everything possible! Maria and Selena found a shelf with some old-fashioned Chinese fans on it.

"Look, Dre," Maria said. "Aren't these fans cool?" She gracefully opened one up and peeked out from behind it, batting her eyelashes. Lil Dre smiled. *Boy, Maria is awfully pretty,* he thought.

Just then, Spooky interrupted Dre's thoughts by flipping open another fan. It had a crouching tiger across the front of it. "Look, Dre," he said. "It's a man-eater!" Lil Dre just rolled his eyes and laughed. Spooky could be crazy sometimes.

"Check these out!" cried Sal. He had found some figurines on a shelf along one wall. "It's a bunch of little warriors made out of wood," he said. "And over here they have all kinds of little dragons, chariots, and horses. I didn't know they had horses in China in the olden days."

B-Down laughed and started rapping a verse:

Yo yo . . . You don't know that, man,
Cuz you don't study in school.
Just dream of skateboarding all day,
You end up an ignorant fool!

"That's enough, Brian!" Señora Campos said. But she didn't have time to say anything else before she was interrupted.

CRASH!

Oh, no! thought Lil Dre. *What now?*

Bennie sprinted from the back of the store and out through the front door like a track star. "Run!" he yelled. The Mijos turned to follow him, and Lil Dre noticed that Bubba was still lingering near the back of the store.

"Hold it right there!" Señora Campos cried. "Everyone, stay where you are."

The Mijos all froze in their tracks, and Señora Campos headed to the back of the store with one of the store clerks to assess the damage.

After a few minutes, she returned and silently led the Mijos out of the store. She was angry! Bennie stood outside the store, with his head hung. His eyes wandered over to Bubba, and he looked like he wanted to explain, but Señora Campos just grabbed his hand firmly and continued walking back to the bus. Lil Dre couldn't help noticing all of the cool places they passed on the way. Too bad they couldn't stop at any of them.

When they reached the bus again, JJ opened the doors and they all filed on. Bubba was the last to board, and he slumped down in the backseat, his arms crossed over his chest. Señora Campos made Bennie sit in the front seat, right next to her. When she began to talk, her voice was shaking.

"I am very disappointed in all of you," she said, addressing the entire busload of kids. "This field trip is a very special opportunity to learn about some new places, and you have shown nothing but disrespect all day. Luckily, the things that Bennie knocked over in that last store weren't fragile, and nothing was broken. But you need to realize that your actions have consequences. We will talk about this more in school tomorrow, but now we have one last stop to make. I expect nothing less than your best behavior. Do you all understand?"

"Yes!" the Mijos chorused.

"Yeah, right," Lil Dre heard Bubba mumble under his breath.

CHAPTER 10

AQUARIMANIA!

The last stop on the Mijos' big field trip was the one they'd been waiting for all day, the aquarium! As the bus pulled up in front of it, the kids could see that the aquarium was really fancy looking. It was a big, old-fashioned cement building with a gigantic shark on top. Wide steps led up to a set of giant double doors. As the kids walked up to the entrance, they were amazed by the size of the shark above them. It had giant jagged teeth and a huge pointed fin on its back.

"Now, that's *definitely* a man-eater," Spooky said. "Imagine if you were on a little fishing boat and it snapped at you with those giant teeth?" He shuddered in fear.

"I wish I had that on top of my house," added Lil Dre. "It's tight!"

After Señora Campos handed out their tickets, the group headed into the main lobby of the aquarium. For a while, the Mijos stayed there, looking at the different displays and playing in the tide pools. The tide pools were pools of salt water with various corals and different critters like crabs and starfish. The kids were allowed to put their hands in the water and touch the animals, which was the coolest thing they'd done yet!

It wasn't long before Señora Campos led the group into a big dark hallway filled with brightly lit aquariums on both sides. The walls of the glass tanks went as high as the ceiling. There were all kinds of fish and other creatures swimming around inside. The information signs read TUNA, ROCK COD, BLOWFISH, SQUID, and OCTOPUS. There was a lot to see, but once Spooky spotted a sign over the entrance to the next room, the kids lost interest.

"This is it!" Spooky cried. "The famous shark room, straight ahead!" There was no stopping them now. The Mijos ran into the next room, giddy with excitement. They'd all heard about the shark room before, and this was what they'd been waiting to see all day!

Spooky ran right up to the glass and pointed at the different kinds of sharks. The other Mijos and Señora Campos were close behind.

A deep voice came from the crowd as a tour guide stepped up next to them. "Hello, everyone, and welcome to the aquarium's world-famous shark room!" he began. "We have several species of shark in this tank: hammerhead sharks, tiger sharks . . ."

If there was one thing Spooky knew about, other than ghosts, it was sharks. He had the whole collection of *Jaws* movies on DVD at home! He peered impatiently into the tank, not listening to the tour guide.

All of a sudden, Spooky cried out. "Whoa! Look at that!" A diver outfitted in scuba gear suddenly appeared inside the shark tank. It seemed like she'd come out of nowhere! She held a large plastic bag in her hand. A whole bunch of bubbles streamed off of her, and the sharks quickly swam over.

"You kids have great timing!" the tour guide said. "You might notice that our diver has a big bag of shark snacks. It's feeding time!"

"What are shark snacks?" asked Mousy. "People's arms and legs?" Everyone cracked up. Mousy was usually pretty quiet, but he was an expert on snacks!

The tour guide smiled at Mousy and continued. "No, the diver is feeding the sharks some shrimp and sardines. They love them!" The sharks now surrounded the diver like a swarm of bees around a hive. After the diver made sure all of the sharks got something to eat, she swam upward and disappeared from the tank.

"Where did she go?" Spooky asked the museum guide.

"She swam up to water level and climbed out using a special hatch," he answered. "When you go up to the second floor of the aquarium, you'll be able to see the hatch there. We keep it locked at all times, and only certified divers can get in." The guide turned his attention back to the rest of the group. "The undersea world may seem cruel sometimes. Big fish are eaten by bigger fish, but that is part of what is known as the food chain."

The tour guide continued on for a bit, and everyone watched the sharks swim by the glass, mesmerized by how big and powerful they were. "Whoa, look at that one!" Lil Dre whispered to Spooky. But when he turned, Spooky was no longer standing beside him. *Where did he go?*

"Spooky!" Señora Campos realized Spooky was missing at the exact same moment that Dre did. "Where's Spooky?" she called.

Just then, there was a huge *SPLASH!* A million tiny bubbles fizzed up in the tank, and the Mijos could see that Spooky was *inside with the sharks*! He must have gone to the second floor and slipped in as the diver came out!

"Oh, no!" cried the guide. He immediately pulled down a lever on the wall. Sirens sounded and red lights flashed. Señora Campos waved frantically at Spooky, motioning for him to swim fast and to get out of the water. All of the Mijos screamed and hollered at him. A shark tank was NOT a safe place to be!

Spooky held his breath and tried to paddle back toward the top of the tank. A huge tiger shark circled him slowly. Spooky waved his hands, trying to get the shark to buzz off. But, of course, the shark wasn't about to leave now. Why would it swim away when it had a full meal right in front of it? Spooky was in big trouble now, and he knew it! He began flailing around wildly, trying to swim toward the surface of the water. The shark was right behind him, and its jagged teeth stuck out, looking like a gigantic saw.

The Mijos stood in shock, watching, and Señora Campos ran up to the second floor. But Lil Dre knew the hatch would have locked behind Spooky, and they'd need someone with a key to open it again. There wasn't time! Before anyone could figure out what else to do, a yell echoed through the shark room.

"Looks like a job for the Big Dog!"

Out of nowhere, Bubba charged the side of the shark tank. He had picked up a chrome rope stand, and held it up over his shoulder. Without a second to lose, Bubba swung the rope stand with all his might and shattered the thick glass. The window made a loud crackling noise, broke into a million tiny pieces, and a tidal wave burst out.

"RUUUN!" screamed the Mijos. They barely

had time to get out of the way before the water burst through the aquarium and out the front doors, onto the sidewalk!

Fish and sharks flopped around everywhere. Volunteers from the growing crowd out on the street quickly helped the aquarium workers gather up all of the fish and put them into emergency tanks in the back of the building, while the professionals handled the sharks. The fire department and police department weren't far behind, and they were all happy to lend a hand. The Mijos, however, huddled together in the parking lot with JJ, waiting for Señora Campos. Was Spooky okay? They didn't see him anywhere!

"Is everyone all right?" Finally, Señora Campos rushed up next to them, taking a quick head count. She had her arm wrapped around a wet, trembling Spooky. He was alive!

"Spooky!" everyone cried. From under his dripping-wet hood, Spooky smiled at them shakily.

"He's fine," Señora Campos said. "But he is in

quite a bit of trouble. Spooky thought a ghost was chasing him, and slipped through the shark tank door to escape. Then he fell into the tank. Now who is responsible for breaking open the shark tank?" She looked around at them.

No one wanted to respond. They were afraid to point fingers at Bubba, but he was the one who had done it, and they all knew it. Would he be in huge trouble? Would he have to work at the aquarium for the rest of his life to pay for the damage? Slowly, all eyes turned to Bubba, but no one said anything.

"Bubba? Was it you?" Señora Campos asked.

Bubba shrugged. "I guess," he said, looking down at his feet.

No one expected what happened next. Spooky ran right over to Bubba and grabbed him in a big hug! "You saved my life!" he cried.

Bubba looked surprised. "You mean, I'm not in trouble?" he asked.

Señora Campos smiled. "No, Bubba, you're not.

You did cause a lot of damage, and we will have to help the aquarium fix the broken tank. But Spooky is lucky that you were there to help him! The divers would have gotten him out eventually, but you thought very quickly."

Just then, a lady with a microphone ran up. A cameraman was right behind her. The reporter stuck her microphone in Bubba's face. "Young man, you're a hero! Can you tell us what happened?"

After getting Bubba's story, and interviewing some of the other Mijos and some of the aquarium officials, the reporter thanked them and drove off. "Be sure to watch the evening news at six o'clock!" she said.

"Wow!" The kids were buzzing with excitement as they climbed back on the yellow school bus and headed for home. "We're going to be on television!" Baby Boy said.

On the trip home, it wasn't long before the

Mijos dozed off, one by one. It had been a busy day! Lil Dre stared out the window, daydreaming. Bubba was the only other kid still awake, sitting in his seat with a little smile on his face.

Señora Campos walked toward the back of the bus and sat down next to him. "Well, Bubba, it was quite a day, wasn't it?"

"Yeah. Yeah, it was," Bubba said.

"Listen, Bubba," Señora Campos continued. "I know that you were responsible for a lot of the trouble that was caused today. While your class-mates should know better than to go along with those kinds of situations, I don't want you to think that you can get away with it just because they're all too afraid to tell on you."

Dre noticed that Bubba looked a little embar-rassed, which was a first.

"I —" Bubba began, then stopped. He looked around to make sure that none of the other Mijos were watching. Lil Dre ducked down behind his

seat, and Bubba continued. "I just wanted everyone to pay attention to me, that's all," he mumbled.

Señora Campos sighed. "Bubba, did you notice how much attention you got when you did something good for someone else?"

Bubba nodded, silent.

"So maybe it wouldn't hurt to do something nice every once in a while," Señora Campos finished. She patted Bubba on the shoulder. "It's something to think about. And you'll have plenty of time to do so in detention this week, with Spooky," she said, and smiled at him.

Lil Dre settled back in his seat. *What a day!* he thought. He had a feeling this wasn't the end of Bubba's bullying. But when he looked back over his shoulder and saw Bubba snoozing in the backseat, Lil Dre thought that Bubba had definitely learned something on their field trip, even if it wasn't about state history.

Dre smiled to himself and closed his eyes. *I can't wait for our next field trip!* he thought.

ABOUT THE AUTHOR

David Gonzales is the creator of the Mijos. He is a cartoonist, illustrator, designer, writer, and family man. He lives in his northern California home with his wife, Eleanor, and his three kids, Monica, Anthony, and Andres, and his dog, Chato.

David enjoys spending time with kids and finds a lot of humor in their faces and in the things they say and do. Having raised three children into their teens, and having about thirty nieces and nephews, he knows kids well — and he has a lot of material to draw from!

UNO, DOS, TRES—MIJOS™!

Find out what's good in the 'hood with the first three Mijos adventures! Join Lil Dre, Spooky, and the rest of the kids as they find fun and friendship in the *barrio*.

❏	0-439-56234-1	Mjios #1: The *Fiesta* Face-off	$4.99
❏	0-439-56235-X	Mijos #2: Save Mijo Park	$4.99
❏	0-439-56801-3	Mijos #3: Spooky's Nightmare	$4.99

Available wherever you buy books, or use this order form.

Scholastic Inc., P.O. Box 7502, Jefferson City, MO 65102

Please send me the books I have checked above. I am enclosing $_____ (please add $2.00 to cover shipping and handling). Send check or money order—no cash or C.O.D.s please.

Name_____ Birthdate_____

Address_____

City_____ State/Zip_____

Please allow four to six weeks for delivery. Offer good in the U.S. only. Sorry, mail orders are not available to residents of Canada. Prices subject to change.

▮ SCHOLASTIC

FEED YOUR MIJOS™ MANIA!

Who Dat? The Official Mijos™ Handbook
By David Gonzales

Who's most likely to build a lowrider? Who eats too many bean burritos? Get all the stats, facts, and secrets on your favorite Mijos characters: Lil Dre, Spooky, Baby Boy, Selena, Maria, and the rest of the kids from Oaktown. Get *muchos* Mijos with the phattest guide this side of Mijo Park!